Root-A-Toot-Toot

Root-A-Toot-Toot

written and illustrated by Anne Rockwell

Macmillan Publishing Company New York • Collier Macmillan Canada Toronto

Maxwell Macmillan International Publishing Group New York Oxford Singapore Sydney

There was a little  who had a little

that went "Root-a-toot-toot!"

The little  who had the little

that went "Root-a-toot-toot!" met a

puppy who went "Bow-wow-wow!"

and they went along together.

The little 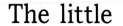 who had the little and the puppy went "Root-a-toot-toot!

Bow-wow-wow!" together. Then they met

a pussy 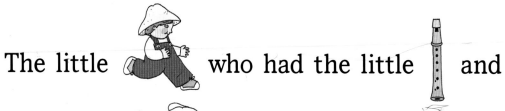 who went "Meow!" and

they all went along together.

The little  who had the little and

the puppy and the pussy

went "Root-a-toot-toot! Bow-wow-wow!

Meow!" together. Soon they met an old,

gray  who went "Hee-haw!" and

they all went along together.

The little  who had the little and

the puppy  and the pussy

and the old, gray  went

"Root-a-toot-toot! Bow-wow-wow! Meow!

Hee-haw!" together. Before long they

met a big 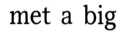 who went "Moooooo!"

and they all went along together.

The little  who had the little and

the puppy  and the pussy

and the old, gray  and the big

 went "Root-a-toot-toot! Bow-wow-wow!

Meow! Hee-haw! Moooooo!" together. Before

long they met a woolly who went "Baa-

baa-baa!" and they all went along together.

The little  who had the little | and

the puppy and the pussy

and the old, gray and the big

and the woolly went "Root-a-toot-toot!

Bow-wow-wow! Meow! Hee-haw! Moooooo! Baa-

baa-baa!" together, until they met a cocky

who said, "Cock-a-doodle-doo! I can make more noise

than you!" So they all went along together.

Then the little  who had the little and

the puppy and the pussy

and the old, gray and the big

and the woolly and the cocky went

"Root-a-toot-toot! Bow-wow-wow! Meow! Hee-haw!

Moooooo! Baa-baa-baa!" and "Cock-a-doodle-doo!"

together. Soon it was time for lunch. They met a

farmer and his wife, who said, "May we come, too?"

And they all went home together.

"Good-bye!"

"Root-a-toot-toot!"